TITCH

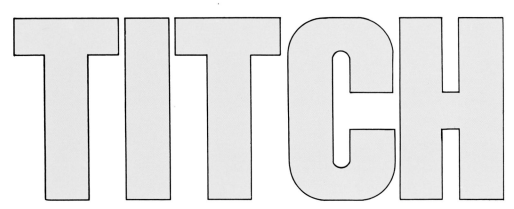

TITCH

by PAT HUTCHINS

RED FOX

Also by Pat Hutchins

Tidy Titch
You'll Soon Grow Into Them, Titch
Titch and Daisy
We're Going On a Picnic!
Rosie's Walk
The Shrinking Mouse
Don't Forget the Bacon
Ten Red Apples

TITCH
A Red Fox Book: 978 0 099 26253 4

First published in Great Britain by The Bodley Head,
an imprint of Random House Children's Publishers UK

The Bodley Head edition published 1972
Red Fox edition 1997; this edition 2002

22

First published in the USA by The Macmillan Company 1971

Red Fox Books are published by Random House Children's Publishers UK,
61–63 Uxbridge Road, London W5 5SA,
a division of The Random House Group, Ltd,
Addresses for companies within The Random House Group Limited
can be found at : www.randomhouse.co.uk/offices.htm

THE RANDOM HOUSE GROUP Limited Reg. No. 954009
www.randomhousechildrens.co.uk

A CIP catalogue record for this book is available from the British Library.

Printed in China

For Darren

Titch was little.

His sister Mary
was a bit bigger.

And his brother Pete
was a lot bigger.

Pete had a great big bike.

Mary had a big bike.

And Titch had a little tricycle.

Pete had a kite
that flew high
above the trees.

Mary had a kite
that flew high
above the houses.

And Titch had a pinwheel
that he held in his hand.

Pete had a big drum.

Mary had a trumpet.

And Titch had
a little wooden whistle.

Pete had a big saw.

Mary had a big hammer.

And Titch held the nails.

Pete had a big spade.

Mary had a fat flowerpot.

But Titch had the tiny seed.

And Titch's seed grew

and grew

and grew.